I0782220

The *Eid* Conundrum

A.S.K. AYNUR

The Eid Conundrum
The Chocolate is on the Wall

First Edition Book, April 2023

Book cover design, illustration, editing, and interior layout by:

www.1000storybooks.com

This book has been inspired by my childhood and is dedicated to my children and grandchildren.

It was late on the Eve of Eid, and Jill the Giraffe was busy in the kitchen.
Tomorrow, Jill was going to throw her first-ever Eid lunch party.
"Everything has to be perfect," she said to herself as she placed her tray of very special Eid pistachio baklava, with melted chocolate drizzled on top, into the oven.

The party was to be for all her housemates.
They had all decided to stay at home this Eid instead of going back to see their families. This was why Jill had worked hard all week.
It was so important to make this Eid one to remember.

It was nearly midnight when Jill took the baklava out of the oven!
"Oh dear," she yawned. "It's so late."
She placed the baklava on the kitchen table to cool overnight and
climbed the stairs up to bed.

Jill woke up very early on Eid morning.
By 6 a.m., she was carefully coating her cool baklava in chocolate drizzle!
She cut them up into squares and they were ready to go.

As lunchtime approached, Jill and one of her housemates, Oliver the
Owl, left the kitchen to set the table.
But when they returned, they discovered something strange.

“There are three baklava missing!” exclaimed Oliver.
“Oh no!” said Jill. “Where can they have gone?”
“House meeting!” Oliver called up the stairs.

Once everyone had gathered in the kitchen, Oliver began the investigation.
“Somebody has snaffled three of Jill’s special Eid baklava!” she said.
“And all that’s left of them are these splashes of chocolate on the kitchen wall.”
“Does anybody know anything about all this?” asked Jill.

"I say it was Camilla the Camel!" said Darrel the Donkey. "She loves your baklava. She's always talking about it!"

"Hey!" Oliver piped up. "I won't have you accuse my best friend like that. Camilla is a good camel. She would never steal, would you, Camilla?"
"No, never," said Camilla. "I love baklava, but I hate stealing!"
But even though Oliver insisted it wasn't Camilla who had taken the baklava, nobody believed her.
"Hmmm. She does love sweets, though," said Herb the Hyena.
"And I've seen her eat things super fast," added Harriet the Hippo.
"She can't resist the smell of fresh baking," observed Sly the Shark.
"Or the taste of chocolate," said Darrel.

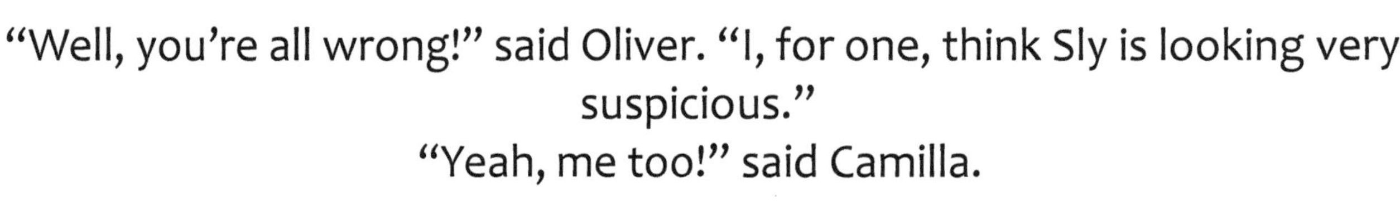
"Well, you're all wrong!" said Oliver. "I, for one, think Sly is looking very suspicious."
"Yeah, me too!" said Camilla.

"How dare you!" exclaimed Sly.
"It can't be Sly," said Darrel. "He used to be in the military. He was an
honorable officer!"
"He'd never dream of it," said Harriet.

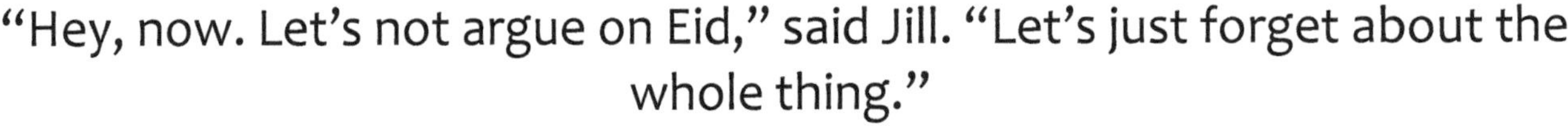

"Hey, now. Let's not argue on Eid," said Jill. "Let's just forget about the whole thing."
And with that, Jill set the remaining baklava on the table.

But when everyone else was in the kitchen, when he thought nobody was looking, Sly the Shark swooped in and snapped up every last square of baklava!

But Sly didn't realize that Oliver and Camilla were watching from the doorway!
"Aha!" yelled Oliver.
"Caught you!" said Camilla.
"We knew it was you!" they said together. "Come look, everyone."

Everyone rushed in to see a very guilty-looking shark with crumbs and chocolate scattered all over his face.
"What do you have to say for yourself, officer?" asked Jill.

"Oh, dear." Sly looked down. "I'm so sorry, friends. I'm so embarrassed. I don't know what came over me… I couldn't resist… forgive my moment of weakness, would you please? And Camilla, I'm so sorry for accusing you. There is no excuse."

Even though Sly had behaved badly, he realized how wrong he had been and apologized. And, as they were friends, they all forgave him. It was Eid, after all!

Even without the baklava, Jill's Eid lunch party was a joyful, delicious, delightful success!
"And for my final gift," she said after lunch, "I shall get back in the kitchen and make a fresh batch of baklava for us to enjoy tomorrow!"
Everyone cheered! They all agreed it was the best Eid ever.

ABOUT THE AUTHOR

Accidental author A.S.K. Aynur is also a speaker and mindset coach. Despite not having the ambition to write as a child, she became a best-selling author in 2020 with her first book.

That she has many strings to her bow is no surprise to anybody who knows her, as she is a serial entrepreneur. She describes her mind as very active and uses writing to get her ideas out and focus her thoughts. Her inspirations come from far and wide—world events, real-life stories, personal experiences, and the work of other writers.

Through her writing, she hopes to impress on readers that, whatever life throws at you, there is always a funny side. Her aim is also to help parents to teach good values to their children through entertaining tales.